THE RABBI *Slurps* SPAGHETTI

By Leslie Kimmelman
Illustrations by Sharon Davey

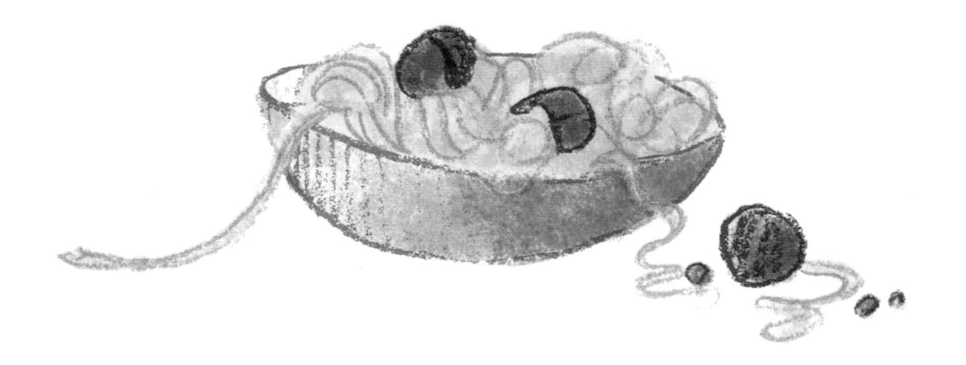

To Marianne, the librarian,
and to Rabbi Billy, with much appreciation.
—LK

For Neve and Alex, always.
—SD

Apples & Honey Press
An Imprint of Behrman House
Millburn, NJ 07041
www.applesandhoneypress.com

ISBN 978-1-68115-543-2

Library of Congress Cataloging-in-Publication Data

Names: Kimmelman, Leslie, author. | Davey, Sharon, illustrator.
Title: The rabbi slurps spaghetti / by Leslie Kimmelman ; illustrated by Sharon Davey.
Description: Millburn, NJ : Apples & Honey Press, [2019] | Summary: Detective-in-training Lena and her dog, Sandy Koufax, investigate how Rabbi Max can do so many different things, from braiding challah to building a sukkah, so well. Includes a note for families.
Identifiers: LCCN 2017059974 | ISBN 9781681155432 (2)
Subjects: | CYAC: Rabbis--Fiction. | Jews--Fiction. | Judaism--Customs and practices--Fiction. | Family life--Fiction. | Mystery and detective stories.
Classification: LCC PZ7.K56493 Rab 2019 | DDC [E]--dc23 LC record available at https://lccn.loc.gov/2017059974

Design by Alexandra N. Segal
Edited by Dena Neusner
Art Directed by Ann Koffsky
Printed in China

1 3 5 7 9 8 6 4 2

Someday I'm going to be a

WORLD-FAMOUS DETECTIVE.

Meanwhile, I'm brushing up my snooping skills. My trusty assistant, Sandy, needs practice, too.

Right now we're working on "THE CASE OF THE MYSTERIOUS RABBI."

It’s a tricky one. The rabbi seems to be everywhere. How can one person do so many different things in so many different places? He never seems to sleep!

It's hard to keep up
with Rabbi Max.

He celebrates *simchas*—like weddings and bar and bat mitzvahs—like nobody else. He's the last guy on the dance floor.

He welcomes new babies
with total bliss.

It's a little
embarrassing.

He teaches Torah to kids and grown-ups alike.

But here's something you may not know . . .

The rabbi

SLURPS

spaghetti!

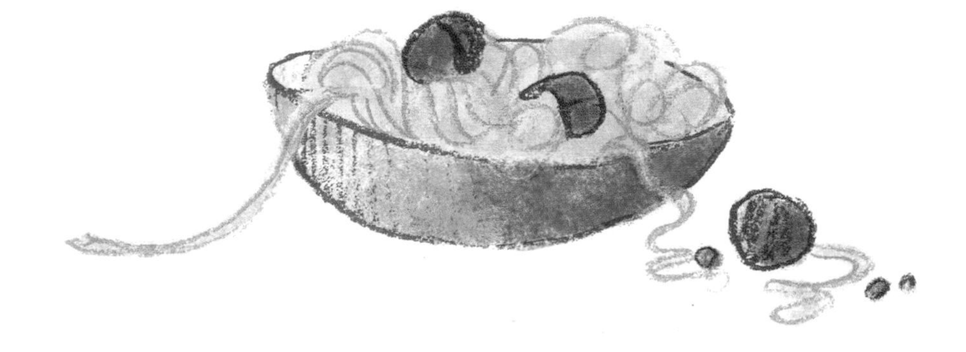

Sometimes I think Rabbi Max

IS A SUPERHERO.

It's a bird...
It's a plane...
It's Super Rabbi!

He's awesome at braiding challah

and spectacular at building a sukkah.

But (and please don't spread this around) . . .

The rabbi
leaves his
DIRTY SOCKS
all over
the place!

At the annual
Synagogue Skate,
the rabbi's moves
are super smooth.

And you should hear him and Cantor Lori sing duets.

But people might giggle if they ever found out . . .

The rabbi
looks quite
ELEGANT
at tea parties!

Rabbi Max is a grill-master extraordinaire
at our annual Shabbarbecue

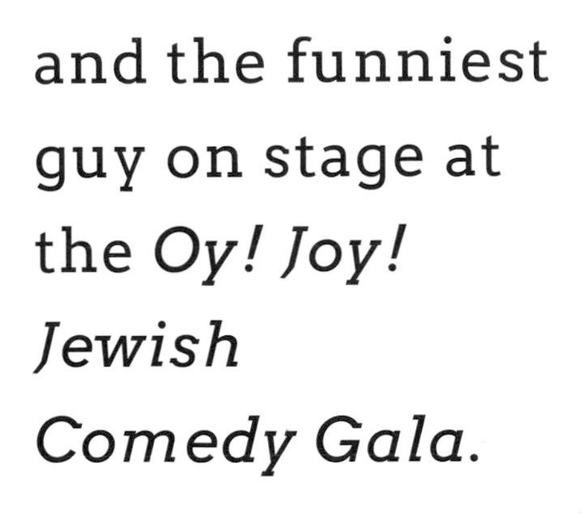

and the funniest guy on stage at the *Oy! Joy! Jewish Comedy Gala*.

BUT SSHH! This is top secret . . .

The rabbi's wife calls him "POOKIE"!

Rabbi Max is the first to volunteer for Mitzvah Day.

He's always right there
when someone needs comforting.

Everyone loves him. You should hear them talk after Shabbat services.

Sandy, I think we've cracked the case.
How does Rabbi Max do it all? At home, in the community,
or at the synagogue,

Rabbi Max is just one

AWESOME PERSON.

How do I know all his deep, dark secrets, anyway? I'm still only a detective-in-training. And I don't have supersonic sight or special long-distance hearing powers.

It's just that every time Rabbi Max slurps spaghetti . . .

I SLURP
spaghetti right
beside him!

Dad,
you have sauce
on your chin.

A NOTE FOR FAMILIES

As Lena learns through her detective work, a rabbi has many jobs! Rabbi Max teaches Torah to the community; leads Shabbat and holiday services; conducts weddings and bar and bat mitzvah ceremonies; gives advice and comfort; helps make the synagogue run smoothly; and participates in every part of Jewish community life. He has a family, too! Plus, Rabbi Max is a *mensch*. *Mensch* is a Yiddish word that means a person of honor and kindness.

★ Which of the rabbi's jobs do you think are the most important? Why?
★ If you were a rabbi, which job do you think would be the most fun?
★ Can you think of some people you know who are mensches?
★ What things can you do each day to be a mensch?

Slurpily yours,